The Piggest Show on Earth

SHOW ON EARTH

by Arlene Dubanevich

TICKETS

Step
right up

ORCHARD BOOKS · A division of Franklin Watts, Inc., New York

Orchard Books
A division of Franklin Watts, Inc.
387 Park Avenue South
New York, New York 10016

Orchard Books Canada
20 Torbay Road
Markham, Ontario 23P 1G6

The text of this book is hand-lettered by the artist. The illustrations are full-color,
with a separate black-line drawing, printed in four colors.

Manufactured in the United States of America.
Book design by Arlene Dubanevich.

10   9   8   7   6   5   4   3   2   1

Library of Congress Cataloging-in-Publication Data
Dubanevich, Arlene.
The piggest show on earth / Arlene Dubanevich.
      p.   cm.
Summary: Two young pigs have an exciting time at the circus when one of
them loses her balloon in the middle of the circus parade.
      ISBN 0-531-05789-5.   ISBN 0-531-08389-6 (lib. bdg.)
      [1. Pigs—Fiction.   2. Circus—Fiction.]   I. Title.
PZ7.D8492Pg   1988   88-11742
[E]—dc19   CIP
                                                            AC

To Mil